Just Plain George

Written by Lori Egan

For those who are lucky enough
to discover, and become part of,
the magical world
of the horse.

Best Wishes
Sori Egan
2006

CHAPTER I

◆●◆

I was quite the athlete when I was younger. I kept up with the best of them. I was lucky enough to be able to travel the country, all over the world, to compete. I even have an Olympic medal. Oh, I have many other trophies, but that Olympic medal is really special. I wasn't supposed to win that one. I was the underdog, so to speak. Boy, did I prove everyone wrong. An Olympic medal–not bad for your average, ordinary horse. That was what I was called: "plain, average, ordinary horse." I guess I was insulted, but I knew better. I knew an average, ordinary horse could accomplish great things. And I did. I had help from my rider, my friend, Jill. She thought I was anything but average and ordinary. My name is George Bailey. I was named after a character from Jill's favorite movie; I never have actually seen the movie. I am a 17.2 hand, bay thoroughbred. I was bred to be a racehorse. 17.2 is pretty large as far as horses go. We are measured in hands. One hand equals four inches. So, I am about five foot eight in people height. Jill and I competed in a sport called Three-Day Eventing. It was all very exciting. I didn't start out as a three-day horse. Before I met Jill, I was in a racing stable. It was hard work. We went out very early in the morning for our workouts. Sometimes it was barely light out. I always did my best but sometimes I would just get tired. I liked my groom at the racetrack. She used to cut up carrots and apples and add it to my meal of oats, barley and sweet feed. The food was really good, they fed us well. In my two-year career at the races I ran eight times. I finished first two times, second once and third two times. Winning was fun. The crowd would cheer loudly as I crossed the finish line. Everyone made such a fuss. After the race, they would put the winner's blanket on me and everyone would gather around for a photograph. I thought my record was pretty good but my owners were not impressed. They thought I was just an "average, maybe below average, horse." I was about to celebrate my fifth birthday at the racetrack when I found out I was being sent to a sale. As my groom led me down the shed row, I said good-bye to all of my friends, who answered as I passed their stalls:

"We'll see you again, Young Fellow," said the lead horse, Rex, who led us out to the track every morning.

"Good luck, keep your chin up," said Winston. He was an up-and-coming star—just two years old.

"Make sure you are on your best behavior," suggested Belle. She was about to retire herself and become a broodmare. I thought she would make a great mom.

I stopped by the stall of my best friend Stitch. He was a very handsome chestnut with the shiniest coat I had ever seen. He had a white blaze and four white socks. He was a champion and looked like one. I would miss him most of all. We went out to the track every morning together. He was much faster than I was, but he never made fun of me because I could not keep up. He always encouraged me to do my best, so I tried hard every morning.

"Remember to be your best, Young Fellow," he said as I stopped at his stall. "I will miss you." I'll always remember you, Stitch. Good luck, I will miss you too.

Stitch had a very successful career. He won many races. I later heard he won Horse of the Year for two years in a row. I was very impressed and I was proud to have been his friend.

My groom led me out of the barn and onto the van. I remember it was a very cold night. I don't think I will miss the racetrack, only the friends I made. I might miss the food though—did I mention the food was really good there? I settled in on the van, I had a long ride ahead of me. It was a pretty bumpy ride, but I had plenty of hay in my hay net and four other horses to ride with so it really wasn't bad. I snoozed a little and ate a lot and it wasn't long before we reached the sale barn. It was morning, so it wasn't as scary being led out of the van, I could get a good look at my surroundings. Some of the other horses seemed sad about being in the sale. Not me. I was going to be on my best behavior, look as smart and handsome as I could. Or maybe I would look cute, cute might work better.

I was put in a stall with water and hay; I was to wait my turn to go through the sale. People walked by our stalls all day; they wanted to look us over before the sale started. Once in a while someone would ask to look at us outside of our stalls. They would trot us up and down the barn, and run their hands over our legs. They were checking for any lumps and bumps. You wouldn't find any on me. I figured out what the people were doing during this process—so as they were checking me over, I was checking out my potential new owners. When I met someone I liked, I behaved like a perfect gentleman. A few people spoke about racing me again. To them, I acted cranky and did not trot my best. I already tried racing, I knew that wasn't my game. I didn't know what was, but I knew I was going to be good at something. Something new. I may have been considered old for racing, but I was young enough for the rest of the horse world.

It was soon my turn to go through the sale. It was nighttime now. It was dark in the waiting area but I could see lights where the sale was going on. Okay, my turn now. My handler led me through the doors to the sale arena. Very bright lights were shining on me. I was a little scared. No one told me there would be a spotlight on me, with hundreds of people staring at me. I trotted in place—that is what I do when I am nervous. As I entered the arena someone knocked over a chair with a BANG! I jumped at that, accidentally stepping on my handler's toes. Sorry about that, I didn't think I hurt him. I didn't think this was a good way to start. I was worried I looked like a fool. The auctioneer started the bidding. Everything was happening so fast. I heard numbers being yelled out, people were raising their hand or yelling out numbers. My heart was racing–people were actually bidding on me! I tried to look for familiar faces from earlier in the day. The man who wanted me to race again just bid on me. The next bid came from the people who said I looked "plain." I was surprised they were interested. Next was a lady who wanted me for something called trail riding; she seemed nice. I was looking for the young girl who said I looked like I could jump big jumps. Now that sounds like something I could do. Where was she? She was with her father. I frantically looked around the arena. The girl had long blonde hair; she had it in a ponytail. I didn't think her hair looked like a pony's tail, but that is what it was called. She was shorter than most humans I had met. Except for the jockeys—she was a couple of inches taller than them. Her father was a tall human with brown hair and glasses. Oh, there they are. Her father just bid on me, I think. I focused all my attention on that girl. I can jump big jumps for you, I promise. I let out a little nicker in her direction, and put on my most handsome look. I thought handsome would be better than cute if I had to do something as important as jump big jumps. I nickered again at the girl—I think that did it. She tugged on her father's sleeve, he raised his hand and there was a loud BANG! on the stand from the auctioneer. "Sold!" he yelled. I jumped, oops, and stepped on my handler again. I thought he would be glad to get rid of me.

Out we went, out of the sale arena, out into the cold night. Jill's father put a blanket on me. Instead of going back to the stall, he led me to a smaller van than the one I came over on. Jill put bandages on my legs to protect them while on the van ride. She patted my neck and led me into the van. That is when Jill and I became a team. And the rest, as they say, is history.

CHAPTER 2

———◆●◆———

I ate the hay in my hay net and slept quite a bit. I was tired after all that excitement. It was daytime when I woke up. I looked out the window of the van as we drove down the driveway of my new home. Big green fields just like the ones I remember when I was a foal. This is pretty nice, I thought. Now where are those big jumps I have to jump? I wonder if I will jump them today? We drove past another ring; it had very colorful jumps in them. They looked fun too. I couldn't wait to get started.

Jill led me off the van. I stood perfectly still while she took my blanket off. "He seems to have good manners," her father said as he walked over to us. He fed me a carrot. "Oh you're worse than me. You'll spoil him," Jill laughed. She led me over to a huge paddock. She closed the gate behind us and took my halter off. I stood for a few seconds, watching her. I rolled a little in the nice dirt—it felt so good on my back to do that. After rolling and covering both sides, I shook some of the dirt off. I walked back over to Jill. Okay, I was ready to jump those jumps now. I stood in front of her. She was laughing. "Go on, boy. Go run around so I can see how you move." She clucked and pushed me away. Okay, I decided to take a look around. I trotted off. It was good to stretch my legs after the long van rides. Yeah, this is good. I started to canter and let out some playful bucks. My paddock was huge! I don't remember ever being in one as large as this. I could really kick up my heels in a paddock this big, I thought. I decided to run a little. I ran a little faster. Next thing I knew I had run completely to the other side of the paddock. I stopped and looked back. Jill and her father were still there. Maybe she wanted to jump those big jumps now. I ran back over to her as fast as I could and stopped gracefully in front of her. Whew! That was fun!

"What do you think?" her father asked.

"I think he is beautiful, I love him!" Jill answered as she hugged her father. "I have a name for him too. George Bailey."

"From your favorite movie. I think it suits him," said her father.

She loves me and thinks I am beautiful. I wondered if beautiful was better than handsome and cute? I think I picked the right owner.

Jill and her father walked away, leaving me in my paddock by myself. Wait, where are you going? What about those jumps? I trotted back and forth in front of the paddock gate. Jill came back a few minutes later with three large flakes of hay. Oh good. I was getting a little hungry. She left the hay for me and cleaned out and filled my water bucket. I drank some while she was filling it. I swished the cool water around with my nose. Oops, I splashed Jill while I was doing that. She wasn't mad, in fact she laughed and kissed me on the nose. She left me alone to eat my hay. I knew I would like living here. Life was good.

I didn't have to do any work on my first day. I stayed out in the paddock, eating all the hay Jill left for me. I rolled a few more times, and made a couple more laps around the paddock. Throughout the day, other horses were turned out in the paddock next to mine. I made sure I went to the fence to greet everyone. I wanted to make a good first impression and hopefully make some new friends. The last horse I met was a very stout fellow, with a beautiful, shiny, black coat and two white front legs. He had been here the most years, I had found out. "So you are the new guy?" he asked. "Nice to meet you. You take good care of Jill. That's your job now. It used to be my job, but I'm semi-retired. Now I teach beginners to ride. I took Jill to her first horse show when she was six. That was 12 years ago. We did many horse shows when she was growing up. I took her to her first three-day event also. Boy, was she nervous. But I got the job done, and got her home safely." Three-day eventing? Is that what I will do? I asked my new friend. "Yes you have lots of training ahead of you. But if you are to stay with Jill, three-day eventing is what you will be doing," he explained.

Oh I wanted to stay with Jill. How do I do this three-day eventing? I wanted to learn everything as fast as possible. "Don't worry, Jill will teach you everything. I taught her everything I know, she's worked very hard. She's a very talented rider. Let me know if you have any questions." My new friend was very helpful. Thanks. I asked him his name. "Everyone calls me Sam." I'm George Bailey, I told him, proud of my new name. Funny I couldn't even remember my name while I was at the racing stable. The horses there just called me "Young Fellow". Except for my groom—she called me Sugar. Actually I think she called everyone Sugar.

It was later in the afternoon when Jill led me into the barn. I couldn't wait to see my new stall. I found it to be quite comfortable, with fluffy shavings to roll in. It had a door that was open on top so I could look out into the barn, which made it easy to watch everyone and see what was going on. It also had a window in the stall so I could see the horse next to me. I was in the stall right next to Sam. What luck! If he taught Jill everything she knows, it will be easy for me to ask him questions, living right next door. I heard the familiar sound of a feed cart being filled. I poked my head over the door. Yup it's feeding time. I let out a rather loud whinny—just in case they forgot they had an extra mouth to feed now. Jill came in with my food. My favorite! Oats, barley, sweet feed, carrots and apples, too. And a couple of sugar cubes that Jill liked to give me. I nudged her shoulder as she put the food in my bucket. "What? Are you thanking me for your food? You are quite a character." She said as she draped her arms around my neck and hugged me. I made sure I nudged her every time she fed me. Yes, I am thanking you.

CHAPTER 3

During my first few months with Jill, we spent a lot of time jumping small jumps, sometimes single jumps, sometimes three jumps in a row (they're called gymnastics, Sam told me). Sometimes we rode in a ring without any jumps at all, it just has some letters around the arena. It is called a dressage arena. That too I found out from Sam. Apparently dressage is one of the things we do on the first day of three-day eventing, then cross country, and then the final day is stadium jumping. Sam told me to pay special attention to Jill in that dressage ring—the dressage score was very important. I hadn't jumped any of those big jumps yet. Sam assured me I would, and to just be patient.

My favorite thing to do was to ride outside in the big fields. That was when I got to see the big jumps. They were beautiful—all natural logs, ditches, water jumps, and hedges. Let me at them! By the springtime, the jumps were getting higher and the work in the dressage ring was getting harder. One day while we were riding out on the cross-country course, Jill rode me towards a new, bigger jump—not one of the really big ones but it was bigger than what we were jumping. We sailed right over it! It was great fun. "See, George is a natural," Jill said to her father as we galloped by.

It was the middle of the summer when I went to my first horse show. It was all very exciting. Jill braided my mane. She was going for the handsome look, I think. Maybe now I get to jump those big jumps. After we had our warm-up we headed over to the dressage ring. I knew the dressage scores were really important, so I listened carefully to everything Jill asked for during the warm-up time. We waited our turn outside the ring. I watched the horse and rider that were going before us perform their test. I paid special attention to the horse. He was a big gray horse, probably the biggest horse I had ever seen. He was really good. He just floated around the arena. I thought he was pretty light on his feet for a big guy. I was getting nervous. Does my trot look that good? What about my canter transition? I think I hop more from trot to canter. Should I change that? I wished Sam were here, he would have told me what to do. I started to trot in place. "Whoa, George, it's okay" Jill said as she patted me on the neck. "We're next." We trotted on the outside of the ring. The judge rang a bell that signaled to us we were ready to go. Okay, three-day eventing, here I come! Jill and I started the dressage test. I tried to do everything perfectly. I think my canter was a little slow; Jill kept nudging me with her leg. I figured that out a little late—we were halfway through the test. I hoped we didn't get a bad score; it would have been entirely my fault. We cantered again, I think this time I went too fast. Jill closed her fingers on the reins and slowed me down. This dressage is hard work. We headed up the center of the arena. We were just about done. We halted and Jill saluted the judge, and the judge saluted us back. Wow, this is fancy, important stuff. I can't wait to jump. We walked out of the arena, Jill gave me many pats on the neck. "Good boy, George, way to go," she whispered. We walked over to where her father was watching. "That was a wonderful test, he looked relaxed," he said. "He was perfect. I think I could have ridden him better," Jill said as she got off and led me back to the trailer. No, you were perfect, Jill. I nudged her shoulder. She gave me a sugar cube. I got a bath, and she let me eat grass while I dried off. Then we went home. I was munching on the hay in my hay net and we were halfway home before I realized I didn't get to jump any jumps today. I wonder why? I'm sure Sam will know. I couldn't wait to get home. I was actually tired from the work I did at my first show. I was getting hungry, too, and looking forward to the evening meal that was waiting for me in my stall at home.

The day after a show or hard schooling session, Jill would take me out for long walks in the fields. We just went out to play, no serious work. I was always alerted to the fact we were to go on a "play" ride because Jill would show up in the barn and have both of her dogs with her. If it were serious workdays, the dogs stayed in the house. I would be resting in my stall, munching on hay, when I would see, no actually I would hear, them first. The dogs would charge into the barn full speed ahead, barking, sending the cats running. There would be dogs and cats scattering in all different directions. It was quite comical. I guess the dogs liked their play rides in the field too. They would run in circles around Jill, barking and leaping in the air. I think they would have done back flips if they were able to. One dog was a Welsh Corgi, Bess. She was a cute little dog, black, tan, and white, with short legs and practically no tail. The other dog was a large black Labrador, floppy ears, large paws and a tail that wagged constantly. I never could get his name right. Ben, or Boots, or Boo. It was something like that. I decided to stick with Boots. Boots was a very goofy dog. He would get himself into all sorts of trouble. It was just because he was nosey. He had to investigate everything. Usually that meant going through some large puddles and muddy tracks. He was the most fun in the snow. He would bury his head in the snow, and tunnel his nose as far as he could go. When he came back up, he had a pile of snow on his nose, and an even larger pile on the top of his head! Very funny dog.

In the summer time, Jill would give me a very soapy bath after our ride. Boots would end up getting one too-depending on how much dirt or mud he got into. He always managed to shake off some of the mud and it would land on Bess. Bess was not at all fond of getting a bath. She would have a very odd just-get-this-over-with look on her face the entire time.

Once the dogs traveled with us to one of the horse trials. I could hear Boots and Bess barking as Jill and I were approaching the finish line of cross-country. They were running and leaping, cheering us on as we finished the course. The next day, when we went out for our play ride, Jill laughed at all of us because we just walked quietly around. No goofing off on that ride. We were just too tired from the work we did at the horse trials. Tired and happy.

It was really fun to be in Jill's barn during Christmas. Everyone met in the barn and exchanged gifts. My favorites were the edible ones. After the party, the kids dressed up their ponies in red-and-green bandages and saddle pads. Some even had red-and-green pompoms braided in their manes. I looked festive in all red bandages and wore a red-and-white Santa Claus hat. Boots wore a hat with antlers on it. He looked very much like Rudolph, everyone agreed. Bess wore a red collar with jingle bells on it. She led the way as we rode through the neighborhood. We stopped at different houses to sing Christmas carols. We were rewarded with cookies for the humans and carrots for their equine friends. At one house it appeared that no one was home. We were about to leave when a dog appeared and sat on the front steps. So, we sang "Jingle Bells" for the dog. I think it was our best performance. The dog thoroughly enjoyed it.

CHAPTER 4

Jill and I spent four years training for and competing in horse trials and three-day events. The horse trials were the one-day version of the three-day events. At horse trials we would do dressage, cross-country and stadium jumping all in one day. At the three-day events, we would compete in dressage on the first day, cross-country on the second day, and the final day we would compete in stadium jumping. Each part of the competition was different. In dressage, there were no jumps. We had to perform a specific test and were judged on how accurate the test was, if we were relaxed, submissive (listening to our rider), supple (like a ballerina), if our gaits were forward and had rhythm. It was much like dancing. Cross-country, that was the part I loved. The big jumps were out there. Water jumps, huge logs, gates, and banks that you had to jump up or they would have a big drop down. It was all great fun. Stadium day was a little tricky. It had beautiful, colored jump rails. I loved jumping them too, but after dressage and cross-country sometimes I would start to get a little tired. Or sometimes, I would still be excited about galloping and jumping on the cross-country course. The jumps in the stadium ring would fall down if I hit them, and I would be penalized. They sometimes also had tricky lines to them. I would jump one jump and there might be five very tight horse strides to the next one, then I might turn the corner and have to take big strides to the next one. It was the final test of the competition so it usually took a lot of concentration and making sure I was jumping in good form, so as not to knock down any rails. Oh, I forgot to tell you too. Both the cross-country rounds and the stadium rounds were timed so I didn't want to be pokey getting around or I would be penalized. It really was a learning experience at every competition.

I remember one time we were out on the cross-country course, we had just jumped a big hedge. Just as we were landing off the jump, a deer came running around the corner at us. It scared me. I went to the left, and Jill went to the right. I wasn't looking where I was going and fell over some logs. Oops, that wasn't supposed to happen. Someone helped Jill back on and I thought we were going to jump the next jump. Jill turned us around and headed back to the barn. That was when I learned there was a rule about a horse taking a fall. You weren't allowed to finish. But I wasn't hurt. It was bad enough I lost my rider—for which I would've just received penalty points. But the fall eliminated us from competing altogether. I walked the entire way back to the barn with my head down. I was sad and figured Jill would be mad at me. I knew Sam would be upset. It was my job after all to get Jill home safely. Well, I knew never to let that happen again. Nothing would scare me on course. I would be ready next time.

We almost had another fall at a different event. We jumped into the water jump. Some horses don't like water, but I do. I loved the big splash I would make when I jumped in. I jumped into the water and it was really slippery when I landed. I skidded forward and lost my balance. Uh oh! I thought as I felt Jill going over my head. I jumped back up and Jill pushed herself back in the saddle. I was relieved. I didn't want to get eliminated and not finish. We jumped the next jump, and Jill pulled me up. Something was wrong. Maybe Jill got hurt? She jumped off and picked up my foot. Jill's father ran over to us. "He is bleeding, he's hurt!" Jill told her father. I think she was crying! I wasn't hurt; I nudged Jill's shoulder. "He is okay," her father said after examining my wound. "It was smart of you to pull up. We want to make sure George is ready for the Olympics." The Olympics?

Wow. Jill and I made it to the Olympics. I didn't actually know what the Olympics were but I figured it was important. Jill's father made it sound extremely important. Sam told me the Olympics were an international competition and Jill and I were going to represent the United States. He told me they were being held in Virginia. I was born in Virginia. Born to be a racehorse. So, I was going home not as a racehorse, but a three-day event horse. I better do well, I thought, my family might be watching. I also wanted to do well because Jill had worked so hard to train me, the least I could do was to get her an Olympic medal. I was going to compete in the Olympics! Imagine that!

CHAPTER 5

I remember the day we left to trailer to the Olympics. It was far from home. We drove a full day. I didn't mind though. Jill always made sure there was plenty of hay in my hay net (it was overflowing on this trip). She also wrapped my legs so I would not bang them in the trailer. Jill's father drove as he always did, and Jill's mother went with us on this one too. She didn't always go on the trips, she said it made her too nervous to watch Jill jump those big jumps. Yes, I finally got to jump the big jumps. Nothing to it. I liked when Jill's mother came with us, she always had extra carrots and sugar cubes for me. Jill exercised me on a lunge line when we got to the barn. It was nighttime, Jill didn't usually exercise me in the dark. I needed to stretch my legs, and I thought it was fun to play around in the shadows. The moon was really bright, and the lights from the barn created shadows. I jumped a few. I spent the night in the barn with the other horses competing at the Olympics. Jill fed me my dinner. I nudged her shoulder. The barn was very busy with competitors and horses. This one must be important because there were photographers and reporters there, too. It was just like at the racetrack when Stitch was running in an important race. I missed my friend Stitch. He would be happy to know I was doing well. And, just like at the racetrack, none of the reporters were interested in me.

I poked my head out of my feed bucket long enough to hear something Jill was saying to her father. Boy, did she sound angry. She was reading from a newspaper, "Plain, average, ordinary horse and an inexperienced rider should be happy just to finish at the Olympic Games, never mind going home with a medal." Jill was furious! I had never seen her so angry. I went back to eating. Jill's father laughed at seeing his daughter so defensive over the article that was written about us. "Now Jill, don't be mad at them," he said. "You and George don't have as much international experience as the other riders and horses." Jill cut in before her father could finish, "You've seen George jump. He is anything but plain or average or ordinary!" I stopped eating for that one, and nudged Jill for being on my side. I had heard those words before. PLAIN. AVERAGE. ORDINARY. *Plain. Average. Ordinary.* I knew we would be great. I wasn't worried at all. I went back to eating, all of this commotion was interrupting dinner. I figured I would join in the conversation once I was done with my food. I had to stop one more time, though. A reporter had come over to talk to Jill. A Nicholas something or other, he said, was his name. He was a tall human, much taller than Jill. He had brown hair like Jill's father, but Nicholas something or other did not wear any glasses. He wanted to know if he could go on the course walk with Jill and write an article about her experience at the Olympics. She told him she would be happy to be part of his article. I finished my dinner without any more interruptions.

The next day, Jill would walk the entire cross-country course, from start to finish. All five miles. I didn't get to see the jumps until the day of the competition. Normally, Jill would come back to the barn at night before I went to sleep. I was surprised that night when Jill's mother came in instead. I looked out to the doorway to see if Jill was outside. "No it's just me tonight, George Bailey," Jill's mother told me as she fed me some carrots and sugar cubes. She gave me extra hay just like Jill would have. "Jill is at a competitor's party (I'd have to remember to ask Sam what that was when I got home). She went with Nicholas. I think Jill has a boyfriend." She said as she fed me one last carrot.

Nicholas the Reporter/Nicholas the Boyfriend. That's okay with me. He wanted to write an article about Jill. Obviously he knew that Jill was a talented rider. If he liked Jill, then I liked him. I slept well that night. I couldn't wait to see what this place looked like in the daytime.

Jill came in at six o'clock in the morning with my breakfast. She cleaned my stall and my water bucket while I munched happily on my oats, barley and sweet feed. She gave me plenty of hay. I swished the water around in my bucket and drank some. Jill patted me on my nose and hugged me around my neck. "You are not the least bit nervous about this, are you? I wish I was as calm as you." I started on my hay. There was nothing to be nervous about; I knew I would do my best.

Jill came back a little later with Nicholas the Reporter. I was just finishing off my hay. Jill put my halter on and led me out of my stall. Nicholas the Reporter held my lead rope while Jill groomed me. She brushed my coat until it was clean and shiny, and picked out my feet with a hoof pick to make sure they were clean. She put protective boots on my legs, then my saddle and bridle. She told Nicholas the Reporter we were going out for a gallop. Great! I love to gallop. One of my favorite things, right behind eating, I think.

There was a nice big field sectioned off as a warm-up area. We spent about an hour in the field, first walking then trotting and finally galloping. When we were finished she asked Nicholas the Reporter to join us as we went for a walk around the outside of the field. Jill always took me for long walks after we did our exercise. I was taking in the sights as we walked. I could see lots of rolling green fields. I thought I could make out part of the dressage arena. It looked like it had a really large grandstand. As big as the one at the races. Wow, it looked like we would have a big audience.

As we walked along, I noticed we were almost at the end of the practice field. At the end there was a paddock, I think I could see a horse turned out in it. Jill was riding with her hands held at the ends of the reins just holding the buckle; she was pretty much letting me walk wherever I wanted to go. So, I headed to see who was turned out in the paddock. I loved making new friends. As we got closer, I got a good look at the horse in that paddock. He was a beautiful chestnut with four white socks. I didn't know many horses with four white socks like that. Only my old friend Stitch. STITCH! Could that be you? I nickered, Stitch, it's me, George Bailey. Oh I forgot you wouldn't know me by that name. "Is that you, Young Fellow?" Stitch asked. It is. It is, I answered. I was so happy I cantered and bucked in place. Oops, sorry Jill. "Whoa, George, what's with you?" she asked. "He acts like he knows this horse," Jill said. Nicholas the Reporter was reading a plaque that was on the fence. He read, "A Stitch in Time. Racehorse champion, two-time Horse of the Year winner. It says he is spending his retirement here at the Equestrian Center." Jill had dismounted and let me walk up to the fence so I was standing next to Stitch. She asked Nicholas the Reporter to take a photograph of us. "You know," Jill said, "I did get George from a sale, they said he had raced before. Maybe he knows A Stitch in Time. I never looked up George's racing record. I should someday." I really wasn't paying too much attention to Jill and Nicholas the Reporter. I couldn't believe I was standing face to face with my old friend. I told Stitch he still looked like a champion, and asked if he liked retirement. He answered, "Yes, retirement is nice. I worked so hard at the races it is nice to be able to rest for a while.

Look at you in your new life. Are you competing here?" Yes I told him, I also told him we needed to do really well. Jill was counting on me. "Just do your best, Young Fellow, I mean George Bailey." Stitch told me, "Do your best, George Bailey." I will, Stitch, I will.

CHAPTER 6

The next morning we were to perform our dressage test. Jill came in to feed me breakfast. While I ate she braided my mane; she had to stand on a step stool to reach my mane. I nudged her a few times; one time I nudged her a little too hard and she fell off the step stool she was standing on. Oops, I nudged her again a little easier this time. I was finished eating about the same time Jill was finished with my braids. She left for a while and I munched happily on the two flakes of hay she had given me. Nicholas the Reporter came in shortly after Jill left. I poked my head over the door. You missed her, pal, but she'll be back soon. I nibbled at his sleeve and he fed me a sugar cube. "Are you ready, big guy?" He asked, "This is it. You look ready. I really want Jill to do well, to go home with an Olympic medal. She deserves it. Take good care of her. I'll be in the stands watching, cheering for you, too."

Hey, thanks, Nicholas the Reporter. Don't worry, I'll take care of Jill. That's my job. I went back to eating my hay. When Jill came back, she was dressed in her dressage clothes: white britches, tall black boots, yellow vest, and black jacket with black top hat. Jill's father and mother were there, too. Her father groomed me, instead of Jill. She was trying to stay clean. Jill was pacing back and forth in front of my stall.

"Stop pacing, Jill," her mother scolded her. "You're making me nervous."

"I can't help it, I have too much energy. I need to do something or I will get nervous."

Jill picked up my bridle and saddle. I nudged her shoulder. I was trying to assure her there was nothing to be nervous about. I got her coat dirty.

"Oh no, let me clean that for you, Jill."

"It's okay, Mom, it's good luck," Jill said and she laughed. "I'd be nervous if George didn't do something to get me dirty." Jill hugged me and put my saddle and bridle on. We were ready and headed for the warm-up area. There were quite a few horses warming up already. I said my hellos as I rode by. There was one gray horse who was a really nice mover, a little skinny though, I thought. You really should clean up your feed bucket, I told him as I rode by. He said something about not wanting to eat when he was nervous. I couldn't imagine not wanting to eat. I hoped that never happened to me. I wished him luck on his test. I hesitated for a moment. There in front of me, was the most beautiful horse I had ever seen. A mare, she was almost all black with a small white star right in the middle of her head. Good luck to you I told her as we passed each other. "Thank you. I go next," she said.

As we warmed up, Jill let me canter around on a loose rein. Then, she took up the reins and asked me to trot and halt, canter and halt; we even got to hand gallop and halt. I think Jill wanted to make sure I was listening. Don't worry, Jill, I was listening all right. We walked over to the ring just as the black mare headed back to the barn. I wondered how she did. We walked to the outside of the arena to wait for the bell. Wow, I looked around. There must have been thousands of people there watching us. This Olympic stuff really is important after all. I trotted in place. Jill patted my neck. I spotted Nicholas the Reporter; he was sitting with Jill's parents right in front. Good, I'm glad they got a good seat. The judge rang the bell. We were ready to go. It was time for us to show everyone that a plain, average horse can perform a dressage test well enough to put us ahead of everyone after the first phase. We were perfect. I just knew we were. Trot—perfect, canter—perfect, extended trot—perfect, transitions—perfect. Perfect. Perfect. Perfect. At least I thought so. From the sound of the cheering from the crowd I think they thought so too. I know we surprised a lot of people with our performance. I wonder if the writer who said that I was plain and ordinary, and that Jill was inexperienced, saw us? I can't wait to tell Sam. Stitch too. I wonder if I will ever see Stitch again? Maybe he could hear the announcer, then he would know. Well, one down and two to go. I can't wait for the cross-country. We headed back to the barn. Jill gave me a big hug. I had worked up a bit of a sweat so I really got her jacket dirty. Jill laughed and hugged me again. Jill gave me a bath and fed me lunch. While I was eating, Jill, her father, her mother, and Nicholas the Reporter were all hugging each other. Everyone was happy. Everything was perfect. Just perfect. I can't wait for tomorrow.

The cross-country part of three-day event is known as the endurance test. There are four parts. We start out with Phase A, roads and tracks. It's like a trail ride and is about three miles long. The second, phase B, is steeplechase. We get to jump a little, usually eight to ten jumps over two miles. Phase C is just like Phase A; we do roads and tracks again for another four or five miles. And then, my favorite part, Phase D, the cross-country phase. We travel about five miles and could jump as many as 40 jumps! There is a veterinarian examination before we start the endurance phase, after the cross-country and before the last day of stadium jumping. They just want to make sure the equine competitors are okay to compete. I don't know if the humans get checked out. Maybe they do too.

For the dressage and cross-country a starting order is drawn, so Jill and I had specific times to ride for dressage and cross-country. I'm glad Jill is in charge of that. I just know to be ready when Jill puts the saddle and bridle on. On the last day for the stadium round we go in order of how well we did on the first two days. The horse and rider who has the highest number of penalties goes first, and those that have the least number go last. Anyway, I had no trouble with the vet exam so I was ready to go. I heard a few horses came up with some problems and had to withdraw. That is too bad, but it is better than horse or rider getting hurt.

For cross-country, Jill's clothes are a lot different than from those in dressage. She wears a polo shirt, a safety vest, white britches, and a helmet with a very colorful cover. Since she was riding for the United States, she wore red, white and blue. I had on protective boots for my legs and grease on my front and rear legs—just in case we hit a jump we would slide off instead of sticking to it and maybe getting hurt. I didn't plan on hitting anything. The roads and tracks and steeplechase phases went off without a hitch. There were so many spectators I could not believe it. Since we did so well yesterday, we really had quite a fan club. I could hear people cheering for us. I wish Boots and Bess were here. This is the first event that I could hear an announcer. There was a great roar from the crowd when the announcer said, "George Bailey has just completed the roads and tracks and steeplechase phases with no penalties." A huge roar from the crowd for me! I trotted in place as they counted us down for the cross-country phase. Five, four, three, two, one—we were off, headed for our first cross-country jump of the Olympics! The first jump had large logs with a huge arch over it. We jumped over the logs and the arch was way above us. The arch had the Olympic rings on it. Everyone applauded as we landed. On to the next jump! I could hear the announcer throughout our ride. I didn't know that each jump had a name. I loved having the announcer guy telling me all the names of the jumps. The names I remembered – The Olympic Arch (that was the first one), The Wagon (it looked just like a huge wagon), Heroes' Brush. It was a huge hedge that sat on top of logs. The logs had spaces between them and I could see water on the other side. I quickened my pace a little; I was excited to be jumping our first water jump. "Whoa, easy George," Jill said as she closed her fingers on the reins. I jumped the hedge and made a huge splash in the water. What great fun this Olympic stuff is! On to some more jumps. I remember the announcer saying we were approaching Beaver's Dam. Beavers? I couldn't see the jumps yet. We turned a corner and there they were, two huge beavers! As we got closer I realized the critters weren't real. Whew, that's a relief. Boy, whoever created them sure did make them look real! We had another water jump to go. We were at The Head of The Harbor. I think it is so cool that all these jumps have names. I couldn't wait to tell Sam. At this water jump, we first jumped logs with really pretty flowers in front of it. We dropped down into the water. I got so excited about the water that I jumped the logs so big I was worried I'd loose Jill. But, she knew what I was doing and grabbed onto my mane before I jumped in. After landing in the water, we got to canter through the water (I think I splashed some spectators), we jumped up onto an island, one more log jump back into the water, then a quick jump back out. Whew! That was great fun. I hope we get to do that again sometime. Jill must have done a great job training me, I haven't had a hard time at any of these jumps, plus I'm not even tired. All that galloping in fields has done wonders. The announcer let me know we were approaching the last jump. That's it? It was called The Old Watering Hole. It had a wooden plank base and the water trough was inside of that–it was filled with water too. I hope no one was thirsty enough to want to stop and take a drink! I saw Nicholas the Reporter, Jill's father and mother on the other side of the jump, right by the finish line. They were waving American flags. I let out a little buck to say hello. And then Jill and I jumped our last jump on cross-country. I bucked and played all the way to the finish. The crowd laughed and clapped and cheered. We were clean for cross-country with no time penalties. We were still in first place! I went through another vet exam. Jill gave me a long bath and rubbed down my legs with a brace that made my legs tingle. But it felt good. We went back to the barn to rest and celebrate. Stadium jumping was tomorrow. I made sure I ate all my dinner that night (like I do every night) and I rested as much as I could. I wanted to make sure I was at my best for stadium jumping. I needed to be at my very best.

CHAPTER 7

Since we had the best score, the least amount of penalties, going into our stadium round, Jill and I went last. For this phase, Jill wore a red riding jacket with a small American flag pin on her collar. She wore white britches and her helmet with a harness. I had an American flag on my saddle pad, and white bandages on my front and rear legs. I think we must have looked great because every photographer wanted to take our picture. Nicholas the Reporter took the most pictures. Remember the beautiful mare I told you about? The one with the white star we met outside the dressage ring? Well it ends up she was in second place, right behind us. Well, good for her, I thought, second place at the Olympics, a silver medal to take home, that is great! The gray horse who was a little on the skinny side? He was in third place, but much farther back. He told me he took my advice and finished up all his food in his feed bucket—he didn't know what he was so worried about before, certainly no reason to be finicky about his food. So good for him too, a bronze medal and he was back on his feed. I had our medals all worked out before I went into the ring for our final phase. I had no idea that the black mare was so close in second place that we could not afford to have even one rail down, or even a fraction of a second of a time penalty. I got all this news by listening to the announcer. Uh oh. Now I am nervous. What if I make a mistake? What if I'm too slow and we get a time penalty, what if I am too fast and take a rail down because of it? I trotted in place and bucked a little, Jill's father was holding me while Jill watched one of the other rider's rounds. She was able to walk the course and have the benefit of going last so she could watch the rounds of other riders. She ran over to me when she saw my little bucking routine. "Oh, don't get nervous on me now, George Bailey," Jill said as she patted me on my neck.

Before Jill mounted, she whispered in my ear. "Don't worry, George Bailey, you have been so wonderful, since I met you even. You made it possible for me to be here. Since I was a little girl riding Sam at my first horse show, I have always dreamed of being at the Olympics. Thank you, George. No matter what happens I will always think you are the best horse in the world." She hugged me before she hopped on. Well Jill, the "best horse in the world" certainly will not let you down. I walked into that stadium ring . . . I was as calm and cool as a cucumber. Not quite sure what cool as a cucumber meant, but I have heard Jill's mother say that about me often. Humans do have a lot of funny sayings.

The stadium course had 14 jumps in it. It was full of very colorful rails and flowers. Jill and I rode in. We halted in the center so Jill could salute the judges. I took a good look around. I don't see anything too difficult out here. I trotted in place. Let's go, Jill. She patted my neck as we were approaching our first jump. It was red, white and blue planks. The second was a white picket fence with white pillars with flowers hanging off of it. That was nice. The third jump looked like an old-fashioned bicycle, the fourth was natural planks with five tight strides to a natural rail oxer. So far so good. We went through the next five jumps without any problem. Jump number eleven was almost a problem. It was off a tight turn, it was the highest jump on course and the top of it was a plank that sat in very narrow cups. Those were the easiest to come down. The crowd held their breath as we went over that—I did too actually. I was glad when we were done with that one. Three more to go. The next one was a big red wall—I like those, no problem there. Now down to the last two. I was getting a little anxious. I jumped in really big. Jill realized this and immediately closed her fingers on the reins to slow me down, she thought we would meet the last jump off stride. I figured I had room for five of my strides until I had to take off for the last one. I started to count. One, two, three, four, Jill had been pulling on the reins trying to slow me down, but I had so much momentum going landing off the last jump, I was like a steam engine chugging through. I had just counted the fourth stride. Jill was pulling me back to add another stride. I didn't think I could fit another one . . . I think we should take off now! I made a huge leap at the jump. The crowd went absolutely silent. Hang on, Jill. Don't worry, we'll make it. It felt like an eternity for us to land. I really put in a big effort so as not to touch that jump. Jill was going home with an Olympic gold medal. We landed and went through the timers. There was a split second of silence. It seemed that everyone glanced at the timer to make sure we made it within the time allowed. We did. We did it! A plain, average, ordinary horse and an inexperienced rider just won the gold medal. Maybe by the skin of our teeth, but we did it. Thank you, Jill, for making it possible for me to be here. Jill received her gold medal; my new friends got their silver and bronze medals. They played the American national anthem, and we got to do a victory lap and gallop around the stadium ring.

CHAPTER 8

—◆●◆—

After the Olympics, we competed in one more three-day event. We traveled to Europe to get that international experience we were lacking. Not that we needed to prove anything to anyone anymore. We were Olympic medalists, after all. Oh, I almost forgot. We won our European three-day event, too. I've been on a bit of a vacation since we returned from our overseas trip. Jill put off going to college to devote her time to training for the Olympics and training me (which I think is a full-time job all by itself.). Jill promised her parents she would finish school after the Olympics. She kept her promise and went to a local university. I'm glad she didn't go far away because I would have missed her. Some days Jill and the dogs come out to my paddock; Jill sits under the oak tree and does her homework. The dogs and I roam about my paddock for a while and then return to the oak tree to keep Jill company. Sam has been teaching Nicholas the Reporter how to ride. Sometimes they come with us on our ride out in the fields. I got an early Christmas present this year. Normally my Christmas present is carrots, apples, sugar cubes, and oat treats. Which is fine with me. This year I got all of that and a great surprise. It was the beginning of December; everyone was in the barn practicing singing the Christmas carols for this year's ride. Nicholas the Reporter came into the barn and said he had a Christmas present for Jill and me too. Nicholas the Reporter led the way out of the barn and into the parking lot. There was a truck and trailer outside. Maybe he got us a new trailer? Then, he opened the trailer and I could not believe my eyes! It was Stitch! I pranced and bucked in place. I nickered to Stitch. Stitch, it's George Bailey. "Hello, George Bailey. This is a Christmas present for me too. I'm coming to live here!"

Jill was hugging Nicholas the Reporter and her parents were laughing and taking pictures. So now Stitch is part of the family too. I introduced him to Sam, and Boots and Bess. Stitch even joined us on this year's Christmas Eve ride. Bess and Boots led the way as usual. Jill and I rode in the middle, with Nicholas the Reporter and Sam on one side, and Jill's father (I didn't even know he knew how to ride!) and Stitch on the other side.

On Christmas Day, Jill came out to my paddock. I thought she came out to study, but she just came to visit. She fed me sugar cubes and hugged me around my neck. "Merry Christmas, George Bailey. I know everyone thought you were just a plain, average, ordinary horse. But I knew you were special the first day I met you." She fed me more sugar. "So, just plain George, I am going to write a book about you. I want the whole world to know how brilliant you are." Jill said as she hugged me. She wants the world to know how brilliant I am? I nudged her shoulder. A book about me. Imagine that.